THE IMPERIAL PORTAL

A NEW AURA OF ADVENTURE

SATYAKI MONDAL

Made with ♥ on the Notion Press Platform
www.notionpress.com

I dedicate this book to my mom and dad for bringing me to this beautiful world

Contents

PREFACE

I am a student of St.xavier's Burdwan and I have always been a bookworm except for my school book. I am a real fan of adventure fiction and reading those dozen stories I felt like writing a story by myself. I felt like creating a new aura for this story so here I am presenting to you my first-ever fiction story "The Imperial Portal". Please enjoy reading it.

Prologue

This story revolves around a 14 years old boy named Luke, who is a student of St.Xavier's School Kolkata. In this story he and his four best friends are together travelling with Luke's uncle Sam who takes them to Goa were he has bought a new bungalow. Read on to find how Luke and his friends find this bungalow as their most adventurous experience.

I

Dream came true

Today is Luke's 14th birthday and he was still sleeping upside down. No one has dared to wake him up from his devastating sleep. But the arrival of his friends was sure to wake him up. It was about 11 AM when his friends arrived, they woke him up with a bucket of ice-cold water. Being soaked with such cold water in summer morning could have been a satisfaction while awake but while sleeping I am not sure whether that would give any pleasure to anyone. Though for Luke the arrival of his friend was a bit sick he enjoyed it later. After having lunch they went to the roof for decorating it with balloons and stickers for the afternoon party. By 5 PM all the decoration was complete and the guest has already started to arrive.

Luke's room was overcrowded with presents of different shapes and sizes. The most awaited thing of the whole party has arrived the birthday cake. It was a custom-made cake from a nearby bakery. It was in the shape of gigantic football with the name Luke printed on it. Luke was wearing his favorite dress a red overcoat and denim jeans pant. After blowing out the candles and distributing the cake among the guest Luke and his friend were allowed to spend some enjoyable moments together. It has been a busy day there wasn't any time to introduce you all to Luke and his friends. They all are from St.Xavier's School in Kolkata. They are a group of four, the most studious among them in Jhon, and the talkative duo are Tracy and Lisa. The bravest was Luke and last but not least the music lover Andy popularly known as "candy".After having their dinner it was now time to return home for Luke's friend but unknown to anyone it was a surprise time for all of them.

Suddenly there was a sound of a car stopping outside Lukes's House. From that particular sound, Luke knew it was his Uncle Sam. Sam is a wealthy businessman and has recently bought a bungalow, to which he is planning to take his nephew along with his friends. Sam banged open the door and entered the house with a gift bigger than himself and was about to fall on top of the shoe rack with that particular gift but was supported by Luke,s dad. As soon as Sam reached up to the roof announced his plan of taking Luke and his friend to his new bungalow. It was the most exciting thing they all have ever heard. The smile on the five friends was like the shining sun. It was Dream Came True for all of them.

(All of the guests have left and now Luke was left with his uncle.)

Opening a packet wrapped in golden foil Luke asked "Uncle where is your new bungalow located?" with wonder waiting eyes. But instead of answering Sam gave him a small card from his purse titled "The Princess Castle". Luke read out loud that the Bungalow was located at Benaulim Beach, Goa. Luke was now full of different questions for his uncle to answer but Sam would not answer a single of them, finally the fight between Luke and Sam was broken by Luke's Mom.

II

The adventure begins

All the packing is complete there are only two days left for their departure. Five of them planned to take a suitcase and a small backpack. Today was their last school day before the summer vacation. They have spent the whole day planning and dreaming about their first-ever tour together. They were traveling from Netaji Subhash Chandra Bose International Airport to Dabolim Airport which will take them about 5 hours. Uncle Sam will be arriving today by tonight and will help them all complete their last-minute packing. They along with Sam have been strictly advised to avoid any kind of unnecessary adventure. Despite such a warning, Sam has promised that it will be an adventurous tour.

(Two days later)

"The clock is ticking fast ,common Luke what are you doing

up there it's about time to leave all of your friends have arrived," said Uncle Sam. Up there in the store room, Luke was busy finishing his last-minute packing which he deliberately kept back for the last minutes. Because the staff which he took were checked by his mother and mother surely would not allow him to take his prank kit which he got on his last birthday. After finishing up the packing of the prank kit Luke Jumped down the stairs straight in front of his uncle who by now would have been on the ground if not supported by John. "Thanks, John," said Sam. They all boarded Sam's white Mercedes and we now finally were out heading straight to Goa and of course, not by car. They reached the parking lot of the airport, parked their cars, and were heading towards boarding their plane.

Completing all the protocols with all those notorious kids wasn't an easy task for Uncle Sam. But Finally, He completed it and was now sitting on a chair waiting for the announcement of their flight he was completely exhausted. Luke has already inaugurated his prank kit by dropping a completely fake cockroach in Lisa's coffee cup. And was now planning it on John who was peacefully reading a noble titled "The perfect murder" with a fake snake. As soon as Jhon saw the snake resting on his shoulder the book went flying and landed on directly Sam's head. Luke was forced to stop all this by Tracy and Andy partially because this was an extreme level of fun and mostly because they feared that the next victim was going to be one of them.

By the time they boarded their flight, the sun was already down. It was about 5 PM now and they will be reaching Dabolim by 10 PM. Sam got the window seat beside him was Luke with his gamepad in hand and beside Luke was Lisa with her camera, behind them was Tracy with her Harry potter Storybook, Jhon with his same book "The perfect murder" and beside him was Andy with his eyes closed and headphones on enjoying the beats of his music, Andy has a real taste for music. About 10 minutes later the flight was high up in the sky. About half an hour later they were served their first meal of the day. It contained Luke's favorite Biriyani and chicken 65 a wired combination according to uncle sam who was much more accustomed to roti and parathas'. Leaving out Sam's rest all others were satisfied with their meal. After the meal, everyone was again engaged in their staff leaving out Tracy who was now asleep.

About an hour later two more of our heroes were asleep leaving out Sam, Luke, and Andy. They were the ones who remained awake for the rest of the journey about an hour before they were to land Lisa woke up followed by Tracy but Jhon was asleep until the plane was about to land. They landed soon after Jhon was awake. And were picked up from the airport by Hari Singh the Caretaker and driver of the bungalow. They were all packed with the food from the flight service so they slept just after reaching "The Princess Castle".

III

The mystery parcel

Andy was the first to wake up he and Luke were roommates for the vaccination so Andy was followed by Luke. They both went to wake up John and Sam with the large blow horn from Luke's Prank kit. The last to wake up was Lisa and Tracy who were terrified because last night they heard some footsteps around their room. Luke and Andy were quite brave they did not believe them but Jhon was terrified to hear it and Sam was busy reading the news paper didnot pay attention to what the friends were discussing. After a bit of argument among themselves about the existence of any paranormal activity in the bungalow Lisa was the first to break attention of Sam. Sam concludes the argument finally by stating that they will be observing it today night from Lisa and Tracy's room.

After having lunch it was decided that they will be visiting the Reis Magos Fort today and then will be returning for lunch. The scenic beauty of the fort was mesmarizing but that did not catch the attention of Luke and his friends rather they found deciphering the Portuguese sign board more interesting, though Jhon was the first to read the Portuguese Luke rather more appriciated for his horrible pronunciation. Everything there was quite eye-catching but Luke and his friend found the cannon second interesting after some sign boards. After spending about 2 hours there it was now time to return to the bungalow were entering there car they found Hari Singh was though on calling him he returned almost immediately

It took them 10 minutes for Hari Singh to return. On returning they found a delivery boy waiting outside the bungalow it was quite strange because maybe it was common for Sam to receive the parcel at his house hardly anyone knows about his bungalow. But with a bit of surprise, he received the parcel it was completely wrapped with sellotape with only the receiver's name and address on it. Coming inside the bungalow the Luke took the charge of opening the parcel if you could call it so, it was empty with just a folded paper inside it. Luke opened the letter

> "*Dear Sam,*
>
> *It is my earnest request to you to kindly empty the bungalow with all your kids or face the consequences. And I promise you it will be hard to bear.*
>
> *Yours friendly,* ***RS***"

All the people inside the room were terrified Lisa and Tracy's jaws fell apart and Sam did not expect to get a warning on his first night stay at his very own bungalow. Andy was the first to speak "No way, we are not going to leave who is this RS ?" before even Sam could answer Luke spoke "we cannot let this guy RS have all the fun" though unexpected John and Tracy together said, "Yes, Uncle,

Candy, and Luke are right". Sam was thunderstruck he was not in a state to give a decision but was forced by children said "ok, but be very careful stick together and measure your steps." After all these the plans for observing from Tracy and Lisa's room were canceled rather it was decided that they will be occupying the living room sofa for sleeping.

IV

Hari Singh

Two days have passed after the arrival of the mystery parcel and Sam has started believing that it was a prank played on him by someone who knows the location of his bungalow. Today Sam has planned to take the children to visit the different beaches of Goa. The first beach was Calangute Beach an extension of Baga Beach it is the largest among all the beaches. Luke and Tracy tried to convince Uncle Sam for parasailing but Sam was not ready to leave any of the kids alone.

Today Sam was driving the car as Hari Singh was on holiday for a week because he said that his mother is sick. Next, they were visiting Morjim Beach the beach surely ranks top among the most serene beaches of North Goa, it also serves as the nesting place where the Olive Ridley Turtles lay their eggs. And according to Lisa, it was her great luck that its the season for the turtles to lay an egg. After watching the turtles it was decided that they are going to have lunch at the Golden Eye restaurant.

The lunch was quite delicious. All were quite tired to move any further so they returned to the bungalow. After parking the car Sam turned towards the bungalow and saw a shadow of someone moving away from the balcony of the bungalow. But he looked again and there was not a sign of human existence so he thought that he maybe was hallucinating because of lack of rest.

(Inside the Living Room)

"Uncle before you whom this bungalow belonged?" asked Andy. Sam said " This one which I have bought is about 70 years standing here from the time Antonio Vassalo the last governor-general of Portuguese occupied India, according to some stories this bungalow was bought by him and after Indian anenexation of Goa he was forced to leave this bungalow in 1961." Jhon asked " how come it doesnot look that old" Luke answered the question "Uncle Sam gave Hari Singh the duty to restore the bungalow." Lisa "How come you know Hari Singh Uncle Sam" "When I bought this bungalow I asked some of the workers to clean it and they found him inside the bungalow and were about to handover him over to the police but I asked him if he would like to work for me and he agreed so I appointed his a the caretaker of the bungalow" replied Sam. Luke asked, "Uncle why was Hari Singh hiding?" Sam replied, "I am not sure because whenever I ask him he refuses to answer." This conversation between Luke and his companion went almost for the whole evening and was broken when Andy while bringing his headphone from his room reported that he saw someone going up the stairs to the second floor and followed the shadow but went there to find nothing but an old door with a peacock feather like handle, he tried to open it but it wouldn't open.

Sam reached out the door to check, he vehemently tried to open it but the door constantly denied to open. Luke spotted that the lock on the door though was built looked to be completely new unlike the door which was old Jhon even called it a primordial door. Been not sure whether Andy decided to leave the matter and so did the other. They went for dinner was everyone felt plagued by the absence of Hari Singh because was the person serving everyone food but today the duty was taken up by Sam and Tracy who woefully messed everything up.

But the trouble for Luke and his companion was not decreasing rather they kept on increasing as there was no news of Hari Singh even though his phone was switched off and Sam never thought of taking Hari Singh's address.

V

News paper

(Three days after Hari Singh disappeared)

Today everything started with little sorrow because under all this tension everybody has forgotten that only one week is left until their return. Last two days they have visited most of the forts at Goa. Today Luke and his friends are alone at the bungalow as Uncle Sam went to find a new caretaker because it has been three days since Hari Singh disappeared and it is becoming increasingly hard for Sam to maintain the house even with some help from the children.

Sam returned by noon without any new caretaker. After having lunch everyone was depressed with the boredom so Sam decided to take them to Benaulim Beach which was the closest but never visited by them. On reaching Jhon and Andy went swimming, Tracy and Lisa started preparing a sand castle Sam was sitting on a chair watching them when it suddenly strikes him where is Luke he turned around and found Luke reading a newspaper it was a strange site that Luke was reading but Sam decided not to disturb him. And as Sam predicted Luke was no more reading the Newspaper and was playing volleyball with others.

By Evening everyone returned completely soaked in water, and too much hungry. Sam took the children to a nearby Dominos to have their evening snacks, on returning Luke showed them something quite alarming as well as interesting it was a newspaper article about a man named Robin Smith who was released from jail on the day they reached Goa. No one noticed anything suspicious until Luke asked them to read the initial of the name RS. Sam instantly denied the guess for RS's real with a prominent reason why would a criminal like to do a crime again just after being released from jail. But Luke drew their attention to the third line "He was arrested at the age of 23 from the Princess Castle near Benaulim Beach on Christmas eve of 1986 for murdering the owner of the bungalow because the owner wanted to sell the bungalow to a promoter. And was sentenced to 60 years of jail." This statement was a shred of convincing evidence that the letter was written by him but still Sam was not ready to accept that the letter was written by the same RS he still thought it was a prank played by someone taking the advantage of Robin's name and relation to this bungalow. Luke was about to argue when the others asked him to leave the matter.

After having dinner everyone gathered in the living room for sleeping except Sam who was still thinking about what Luke said the question was revolving in his mind "Is RS Robin Smith ? or Is how he not able to spot what Luke is trying to say?" Sometimes it also came to his mind isn't he putting these children in danger by allowing them to stay isn't he supposed to send them back home to the safety of their parents what would he answer if something happened to anyone of them? Will anyone spare him for his terrible mistake? Or should he keep faith in Luke and his friends?

All these questions were struggling in his mind for an answer, he was starting to feel helpless.

On the other hand, the same kind of battle was going on inside Lukes's mind, is he supposed to belive what his uncle is saying, is it not convincing enough with all the proof that Robin is RS or is he thinking too stressed himself for an easy conclusion, after all, it is the human instinct to take the easiest path. Sitting in one corner of the living room he is occupied by all these thoughts the dark corner was making him focus more on this Imperial building making him think more and more about what could have happened in this bungalow before his uncle bought it.

VI

Basilica of Bom Jesus

Last night has been a painful struggle inside Sam's mind but finally, he has concluded to let faith decide what will happen to them. Luke has also concluded to enjoy the last six days of his vacation with his uncle and friends rather than thinking about all this RS stuff. So today it was planned that they will be vising the Basilica of Bom Jesus. As planned after having breakfast at a nearby restaurant they went to visit the church. The alluring architectural beauty of the church was heart-touching just like every other visitor Luke and his companions were spellbound by this beauty.

While watching the relics of St. Francis Xaviers on the opposite side of the relic Uncle Sam and Luke both saw Hari Singh and Hari Singh also saw them and began to run away hastily towards the exit behind him was Sam and Luke they were confused why was Hari Singh running but they were surely going to catch Hari Singh. The others were also running behind Luke because they were afraid that they will lose track of Luke and Sam. Finally, they all came outside the church but Hari Singh's speed was too much for both Luke and Sam to chase. All of them were devastated due to running but still were confused about why Hari Singh was running.

Luke said "I was so close to him I even grabbed his back pocket but I missed him. Lisa said "I thought you would catch him because, after all, you came second in the interschool sprinting competetion". Sam still confused said, "let's go back to the bungalow and have our lunch after that we plan to go next." The Basilica of Bom Jesus was quite beautiful but it was the luck of Sam and Luke to enjoy it so they had to go back.

(dining hall of the bungalow)

"Uncle do you think Hari Singh is hiding something from us?" asked Andy putting a big slice of chicken in his mouth. Sam replied, "I'm not if he hiding something but he is surely hiding from us." Luke finishing his glass of water asked "is he trustworthy as much as you think him to be?" Jhon supporting him said, "Yeah, I also doubt that."Sam unconvinced said "maybe."

After having lunch all of them gathered in the living room to sleep except Sam who went upstairs to the peacock-handled room it was too calm and cold without any proof of human existence standing there he thought "something is going on in Goa and though unwanted they getting involved in it". Checking the door for the last time he came back to the living room to find everyone waiting for the next day's plan. He declared next day we will be going to visit Dudhsagar falls.

VII

Water Falls

Sam was the first to wake up. After waking up he woke up the other kid today they are visiting the Dhudsagar waterfall which is quite far away from their bungalow. There was no time for lunch as the safari from the Mollem National Park begins at 8 AM and it's already 6 they will need about two hours to reach there so Sam told them that they will be having breakfast at a roadside restaurant. Before reaching the National Park they had breakfast.

After booking the safari vehicle as Sam's car wont get up the mountain, Sam asked them to wait for the arrival of the car. Soon the car arrived from the driver they got to know that it will take about an hour to reach the waterfall.

(1 hour later)
Finally, after an hour they reached the waterfall's viewpoint and the wait for an hour was worth it the white color on the waterfall gave it the divine elegance to be called Dudhsagar or the sea of milk. The exquisite waterfall with its roaring sound was a living example of beauty on earth. It is part of

the Mandovi river which mixes with the Arabian Sea. Sam said, "after being the largest waterfall in India it should be given the title of the most beautiful one". After watching the Dudhsagar it was time to return everyone was mesmerized by the scenic beauty of Goa they could never imagine without seeing Goa that leaving out its seas it's other beautiful features are enough to call it India's one of the most alluring states.

After having lunch it was time for a small surprise for Lisa it was her 14th birthday so Sam took them all to a beachside resort for cutting the cake so that could Lisa could inaugurate her 14th year. The celebration went on for the whole afternoon and they returned to the bungalow by evening. everyone was too tired to even visit the nearby beach, but as soon as Sam offered for watching a movie everyone was ready to go. It was a show for 7:30 PM they all reached 15 minutes before so they bought some popcorn and were ready for the movie to start. It was over by 10 PM so they returned to the bungalow and everyone straight went to bed or better to say the sofa.

VIII

Attack

"Good morning everyone," said Sam at the dining table sitting down for breakfast. After having a look at all the faces around the table he asked "where is Luke?" "He told us not to disturb him, he is sleeping" answered Lisa. "Mostly he is the first one to wake up what happened to him today?" asked Andy. "I was a little more sleepy today I don't know why" answered Luke entering the room and sitting down for breakfast. "So what's the plan today," asked Tracy. "I was thinking to take you...what happened to your finger?" asked Sam. "Nothing serious, just a cut" answered Luke struggling with his finger to eat. "That seems to be serious!" exclaimed Jhon. "It's okay Jhon he said nothing serious" answered Sam. "I was planning to take you all to Baga Beach today."

(At the Baga Beach)

All the people went swimming except Luke who said he wasn't in the mood to go swimming and seemed to be engaged in some deep thoughts. Lisa asked Andy "what happened to Luke he seems to disturb by some matter?" "Nope" replied Andy throwing the beach ball at Jhon to knock him down. finally, after being requested a thousand times by all of his friends Luke came and joined them. Luke was like the energy supplier for the whole group but as today he was out of energy every one seemed to be lacking energy. Even after the failed tries of Sam and Jhon to encourage everyone up none of them were willing to go Scuba diving.

Sam was getting the whiff that something was wrong with Luke but before he could reach for discussion with Luke someone in a black jacket stabbed Sam with a knife and ran away Andy tried to catch him but he was far away by that time. Everyone except Luke was horror-filled expressions on their faces Luke's face was filled with a distant kind of angry expression which was even fearful to look at but he carefully carried his uncle to the nearby hospital wing with some help from the lifeguard. Until afternoon everyone waited there until when Luke came out with Uncle Sam been treated well and was now able to walk on himself. They all returned to the bungalow.

(Inside the living room)

Everyone was sitting quietly and were joined by Rabi the sub-inspector of Goa police. Rabi was the first to speak "why didn't you contact me Sam on reciving the letter from that suspicious RS". Before Sam could reply Jhon said "Yes, RS, I found another letter from him were uncle was stabbed."

> "*Dear Sam,*
>
> *I thought you would take my warning seriously but you didn't. This is not my warning this is ultimatum or next time you all will be dead*
>
> *thanking you, Yours friendly* ***RS***"

Everyone was already terrfied except Luke who still had same kind of anger and this was a add-on to both of them.

Lisa even started crying in fear but was assured by Rabi that they were all safe now there is nothing to worry about. Now for the first time Sam spoke "I know that was Hari Singh who stabbed me he wishpered in my ear **beware** I surely identified the voice".

IX

The last run

Tracy and Lisa were about to protest when Luke spoke for the first time "you are right uncle Hari Singh is the one who wanted to kill you and us from the beginning". Andy asked "how do you know?" "Yes, how do you know Luke," asked Rabi. Luke without saying anything dashed toward the door and said: "common follow me". Everyone followed him up to the staircase finally Jhon unable to resist his temptation asked: "where are we going?". "Upstairs" was the simple answer given to him by Lisa. They went to the second floor with the room with the peacock feather door.

Luke said, "I need all of your help to break this door." "Everyone together," said Rabi, and instantly everyone kicked the door. It was more than enough to break the door it blasted open. The interior of the room was covered in darkness. At first instant the room occurred to be empty when suddenly someone jumped over Sam, Luke was no more sustaining his anger he punched him directly in the face. The man crumpled with pain. In a trice, Hari Singh jumped over Luke taking him down to the ground but at that time Rabi's punch came directly flying into his face, he moaned with pain and fell to the ground. In the blink of an eye, they were tied up by Lisa, Tracy, and Jhon. They were still grumbling with pain and anger but Andy Luke and Rabi"s strong hands were enough to hold them.

Rabi called his force and soon both the man was arrested and identified one was Robin Smith the suspected RS, he was identified by a local constable and the other was Hari Singh that was known to all. Luke asked Rabi "can you lend me some time before taking them to jail I have something to talk to you all about?" Rabi said "sure". Everyone was seated in the Living room joined by Robin and Hari both handcuffed. Luke spoke directly to Hari "what is your name?" Hari replied "you know I am Hari Singh." "No you are not" answered Luke with a note of anger in his voice. "What do you mean," asked Sam to Luke. "He is Ryan Smith brother of Robin Smith they are who kill Mr. Samuel the previous owner, Robin got caught but Ryan was saved, he stayed here until my uncle bought it, am I right Ryan," asked Luke. "Yes" said Ryan. "But how do you know," asked Lisa. "It all goes back to yesterday night....." answered Luke.

X

Luke's Key

(Last night)

Laying down on his couch Luke's mind was occupied with thoughts of the last 10 days they have spent so many beautiful days together. Again the thought of RS was filling his mind and then suddenly he thought about how Hari Singh related to it but Uncle trusts him and so should we. Or, is uncle too lenient towards him? Is uncle even taking these incidents seriously or is he himself becoming unnecessarily serious about this matter? While he was thinking about it he heard some footsteps outside everyone seemed to be sleeping, he decided to check.

Passing Uncle Sam Luke came to the door of the living room and very silently opened it it was dark outside but in the faint light of the moon, Luke could make out a figure standing in front of the stairs leading to the second floor Luke slowly moved closer to the person and hid behind the pillar just on time to be not noticed by another man who came downstairs. The man spoke, "yeah, I have cross-checked they are all asleep". Luke had no problem identifying the whisper it was Hari Singh but who was the other person was he hiding inside the room on the second floor? There is only one way to know and that is to follow them. They went straight to the second floor Luke followed them. It was pitch dark Luke cannot make out, particularly anything, not even the stairs but he can hear whispers up the staircase. And then he heard a door creaking open and close with a sudden bang.

Somehow he knew that the path was now unnoticed by anyone he could move to the second floor. The darkness of the floor was now cleared off by the light from the only room up there the room with peacock-handled door through its haisy cracked glasses Luke can see the two men sitting facing each and speaking about something which unfortunately wasn't reaching him. He was soon able to make out which one of them was Hari Singh but still he was not able to find out who the other one was. Luke waited for their watching the two people speak without any sound, He was waiting there for maybe half an hour or maybe an hour when he suddenly made it out that the blurry figures were now arguing which was reaching his years a clear whisper. He heard Hari Singh say "No, I cannot let them find out what we were hiding here for more than 50 years now.".Other person now spoke "*Eu entendo Rayan, você não pode se dar ao luxo de ceder o que o pai pediu para você proteger, mas não podemos matar mais pessoas que chamarão a atenção de mais e mais pessoas, como quando matamos o Sr. Samuel.*" Luke was too thunderstruck with the consecutive shocks of Hari Singh being addressed as Ryan, someone unknown discussing the life killing of someone called Samuel but still he kept silent. Hari Singh or maybe Ryan spoke " ok, but what if they found us what if they call the police what if the Imperial secrets are open. They will confiscate all they will take all those secrets this portal has kept secure." Luke was by now spell bound he stuck his ear closer to the door when all of a sudden he heard footsteps coming straight toward him he silently moved away, immediately the door creaked open all lights were off it was pitch black but may staying for so much time in the darkness Luke could make out Hari Singh going out of the room and the room getting locked again. Hari Singh or Ryan went downstairs.

Luke was paralyzed by fear, he remained there may be for ten minutes without any movement when he swiftly came back to his senses and slowly went down back to the living room and closed the door of living room firmly, and went to his couch experiencing a mind strom about what to do next. On laying down and relaxing for a bit he realized that his index finger has got a deep cut and is now burning with pain. He tried but failed to remember how it happended may be when

I understand Rayan you cannot afford to giveway what father has asked you to protect but we cannot murder more people that will draw the attention of people more and more people just like when we murdered Mr. Samuel.

XI

True Story

"That's all happened last night" finished Luke. "Why didn't you call us," asked Sam. "Later, Uncle, first I need to finish the part with Ryan. So what are you hiding from us? and do not try to lie " strictly said, Luke. Ryan spoke "This building was built by Antonio Vassalo during the last of Portuguese reign he named it The casa da praia meaning the hotel by the sea. He appointed our father as the caretaker of this house but in 1961 Indian army attacked and killed Antonio Vassalo and the house was left to my father, All the Portuguese were forced to escape but before escaping my father managed to write a letter to my mother I still have it you can have look in my left pocket" Rabi took it out.

> "*Dear Marlo,*
>
> *I along with the other slaves were forded to live the cas de praia but ever if you come to visit it do check the single room on the second floor with a peaacock handle I made myself befor my lord Antonio went to fight with the Indian army he gave me the duty t hid the imperial treasure that the*

portugese left behing after they were forced to leave India. That may be helpful for you to grow up Ryan and Robin but if you never whish to use the money which I am sure you will. Then tell the boys that I have assingned them the duty to protect the treasure and use it if they need thank you. Give them my love I hope that someday I meet him.

Thanking You

Alexander"

"bem, espero que você tenha sua resposta; que sua alma descanse em paz" said Robin. "well I hope you got your answer; may his soul rest in peace" translated Jhon. "See he didn't write the letter because he cannot speak even English," said Luke. "Then who wrote it?" asked Sam. "Ryan Smith or Hari singh" replied Rabi. "yeah," said Luke.

"Thank you Rabi Uncle" said sitting down with relief of been able to share everything. Rabi now turning to Rayan said "is the treasure still there?" "Yes" answered Rayan. Lisa and Tracy together said "Uncle Rabi can we please see it." "Yeah why not. I hope you dont have any problem Rayan" answered Rabi. Rayan nodded his head.

They all went up to the second floor and then asked Rayan for the location. Rayan went to the table and asked Rabi to remove it and pull the floor up. As Rabi pulled it up tones and tones of glistering gold coins revealed themselve. Luke amazed by the beauty said looking once at the gold coins and then at the broken door " THE IMPERIAL PORTAL."

XII

The adventure ends

Rayan and Robin were taken upto jail soon after the dicovery.

(4 days later)

Today it was the day for the return of Luke and his companions back to Kolkata they woke up early flew back to kolkata on the way they decided not to inform anyone about this inccident. But Luke asked "what about the gold coin" "Rabi asked me to take 25% as offered by government for finding a national treasure but i refused to take it" answered Sam with a smile.

XIII

A year Later

Its Luke 15th birthday unlike luke's last birthday Uncle Sam isn't late this time he on time. And ofcourse with a new surprise for Luke and his friends. Maybe a new trip.

DISCLAIMER

All the historical events noted here are imaginative they are not based on real historical events.

9 798889 863779

Printed by Libri Plureos GmbH in Hamburg, Germany